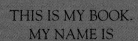

THIS IS MY BOOK.
MY NAME IS

_____

Presents from Pooh

by Isabel Gaines   illustrated by Josie Yee

Random House 🏠 New York

Copyright © 1999, 2001 by Disney Enterprises, Inc. Based on the Pooh stories by A. A. Milne (Copyright The Pooh Properties Trust).
All rights reserved under International and Pan-American Copyright Conventions. Published in the United States by
Random House, Inc., New York, and simultaneously in Canada by Random House of Canada Limited, Toronto, in conjunction with Disney
Enterprises, Inc. Originally published in slightly different form by Disney Press in 1999 as *The Giving Bear.*

Library of Congress Catalog Card Number: 00-107387   ISBN: 0-7364-1106-2

www.randomhouse.com/kids/disney   www.disneybooks.com

Printed in the United States of America   January 2001   10 9 8 7 6 5 4 3 2 1

JELLYBEAN, RANDOM HOUSE, and the Random House colophon are registered trademarks and the Jellybean Books colophon
is a trademark of Random House, Inc.

"Umph!" grunted Piglet as he pulled his heavy wagon. He let out a big sigh as he stopped in front of Pooh's house and knocked on the door.

"Hello, Piglet," said Pooh as he stepped outside. "What's in your wagon?"

"Things from my house that I don't need," answered Piglet. "I'm giving them to Christopher Robin."

Just then, Tigger bounced up to Pooh and Piglet.
Tigger also had a wagon full of things.

"Are you giving your things to Christopher Robin,
too?" asked Pooh.

"You betcha!" answered Tigger. "That way he can
give 'em to someone who needs 'em."

Piglet turned to Pooh. "Do you have anything you don't need anymore, Pooh?" he asked.

"Let me think," said Pooh. He scratched his head and raised one eyebrow. Pooh thought very hard, but he couldn't think of a thing.

When Christopher Robin showed up, he was very happy to see his friends' full wagons. "Are you going to add anything, Pooh?" he asked.

"Oh, bother. I don't believe I have anything to give away," Pooh answered sadly.

"There must be *something*," said Tigger.

Piglet had an idea. "Let's look in your cupboard," he suggested. "There might be something there."

Everyone went inside Pooh's house. Pooh walked straight to the cupboard and opened the doors.

Christopher Robin, Tigger, and Piglet could not believe their eyes.

Pooh's cupboard was stuffed with twenty honeypots!

Christopher Robin took a closer look. "Only ten
honeypots have honey in them," he said.

"I keep a large supply of honeypots at all times," explained Pooh.

"Why is that, Pooh Bear?" asked Christopher Robin.
"Just in case," replied Pooh.

Piglet's knees started knocking together. "In c-c-case of what?" he asked, even though he was a little afraid to hear the answer.

"In case I find some especially yummy honey," Pooh
said. "I would need lots of pots to store it in so I would
never run out."

Christopher Robin laughed. "All honey tastes yummy to you!" he reminded Pooh gently. "Ten pots are more than enough, even for a very hungry bear."

"But what if I had a party and everyone wanted some honey?" asked Pooh.

"If you had a party you would invite everybody in the Hundred-Acre Wood, right?" Christopher Robin asked.

"Of course," answered Pooh.

Piglet quickly counted the number of friends. "Ten honeypots would hold more than enough honey for all of us," he told Pooh.

Pooh still wasn't sure he wanted to give away his honeypots. But Christopher Robin helped Pooh see that it would be a very nice thing to do.

"Think of how many others could enjoy some honey if you shared your honeypots with them," said Christopher Robin.

Pooh began to smile. "Then they would all be as happy as I am!" he said.

Pooh quickly agreed to give away some of his honeypots.

Pooh's heart felt extra big as he, Piglet, Tigger, and Christopher Robin placed the honeypots on his wagon.

"Since sharing makes everyone feel good," Pooh told his friends, "I'm going to do it a lot more often!"

Jellybean Books®

Is your child ready to read?
Move on up to Step into Reading® Books!